UNLOCK YOUR DREAMS

by

Bernie De Souza

DEDICATION AND ACKNOWLEDGEMENTS

This book is dedicated to my two great sons

Luke & Josh

The preparation of this book really has been a team effort. I am extremely indebted to all the friends who have helped, directly or indirectly, with their comments and encouragement.

FOREWORD

E-commerce has had a tremendous impact on the lives of so many people. We have met many of them in our training meetings around the world. This story by Bernie De Souza shows how a young couple learned and practiced the skills that led them to a great success. They faced many of the same challenges that we all have. At times they had doubts and were discouraged but one thing was certain for them, in spite of everything, they did what was necessary. They persevered, followed the business system and did not quit. The result; they unlocked their dreams.

We teach and write about communication and sales techniques in business. These skills apply equally well in e-commerce. Bernie has skilfully woven some of these techniques into this story so that you, the reader, can benefit. By simply making a commitment to studying and practicing these skills you will be amazed at how your business will grow to levels that you could never have imagined.

We wish you every success as you step out on your journey in your own business.

Allan & Barbara Pease
Best selling authors and motivational speakers
www.peasetraining.com

CONTENTS

INTRODUCTION

Read this gripping story of how a young couple, Paul and Hannah, built a very successful business from the seed of an idea. They lived quite ordinary lives until their friend, Mike, introduced them to a business concept. Mike led them through a business plan using a simple pamphlet. From that meeting the story unfolds of how Paul and Hannah went on to develop a successful international business using this model. It shows how they faced, and overcame, various challenges on the way.

Success principles are timeless. Through the generations countless people, from all walks of life, have used them in business and their everyday lives. As you read through Paul and Hannah's story ask yourself the question: "Why Not Me?" Well, we ask you too: "Why not you?"

Can dreamers really succeed? Mike, Paul and Hannah have; they unlocked their dreams. But what about people in the real world like you and me? The answer is an emphatic "YES". You can succeed as you use the principles described in this book. If you know what you are looking for, use a proven business model, set your mind on success, and have the support and encouragement of other successful people, then you too can succeed.

This story is based on a real couple. Paul and Hannah own a successful international business and are in demand to teach people at business training meetings all over the world. Their story will help to inspire you to do the same.

Paul is now a successful leader and motivational speaker. He is sought-after in many countries. Through his business he has developed many friendships across the globe. You too can unlock your dreams.

1 THE INITIAL CONTACT

Paul, the eldest of four children was born in Liverpool. He lived on a rough council estate. His parents split up when he was still quite young. It is easy for anyone to blame their circumstances or their background and to make excuses why they didn't have a good start in life. One thing was certain for Paul; he knew he wanted to make money somehow. He had no clear plan for achieving his ambition; but his burning desire was to progress beyond his status at that time. He was determined that nothing would stop him in his search for a better life.

Paul knew he was academically able but he disliked school, although he loved sport because it gave him recognition within his peer group. Through sport he was allowed to skip lessons to play football for the county.

He left school at sixteen, without any qualifications or any particular career ambition. He applied for a four-year apprenticeship in a small engineering company. On his first day he walked into the workshop and felt how drab and depressing the work benches were. There and then it dawned on him that this was not the way he wanted to develop a life-long career. Paul spoke to one employee who had worked there for twenty five years. He asked him whether he enjoyed the work. "What do you think?" was the reply. Paul walked out that day and never returned.

Paul knew he had to get a job. This was the only way he knew he could earn a living. He mused to himself, "What do I like doing best?" The only answer had to be sport. It was then that he joined a sports course at the local college. While he was at the college he met Hannah who was to become his wife.

When Paul left college he tried various jobs; the first being a temporary one in an egg factory. No matter how often he washed himself he still smelled of eggs. He resented his predicament and felt that, after spending 12 years at school, there must be more to life than this routine. Was this what life was about? Again, Paul concluded that such work would not take him towards his ambition. He decided to join the Air Force, intent on being a physical training instructor. Many of his friends tried to put him off by asking: "Don't be silly, why do you want to do that?" He soon learned that his friends wanted him to get ahead but not ahead of them.

Hannah left college at about the same time as Paul and went into a variety of jobs. Her first position was as a cleaner in a factory. She hated the work and soon moved on to a company that manufactured vehicle parts. This really was Hannah's idea of a dead-end job. She left and became a receptionist in a surgery but, again, it was only temporary. Then she worked as an assistant in a hardware shop before joining the Local Government as a clerk.

Having joined the Military the months and years seemed to pass. Again, Paul found that it was not leading him to the life he yearned. He found that the extra duties, including manning the camp gate and what seemed like endless hours of administrative work, were filling his time. Very soon he realised that more and more of his time was spent on such responsibilities, crowding out his real pride and joy; teaching and participating in sport. He could not see where he was going. So, there he was in the military and Hannah in a job she really did not enjoy.

They decided to improve their income by investing in property; their first house. The bottom end of the market was their price limit so they had to settle for a very small run-down place. They worked hard to turn it into a home. To their amazement, its value doubled in six months, so they bought a second one. Then they decided to marry. On returning from a honeymoon in the Caribbean they let the two houses and chose to live in married quarters. At that time in his life Paul would not have been interested in considering another business or career opportunity. They thought they were living their dream: people were jealous of them, as they appeared to have everything.

Then the property bubble burst. Three things conspired against the young couple. The mortgage interest rate went up, the tenants had "done-a-runner" leaving Paul and Hannah with massive bills and two empty houses. Paul was posted a long way from home to a camp in Yorkshire. Consequently within six months they were heavily in debt.

Then, unexpectedly, Paul met an old school friend.

Paul recalls: "I was just coming away from watching my local soccer team's home match when someone tapped me on the shoulder. To this day I still remember our conversation."

"Paul Evans?" a voice enquired. "Yes. Well! Hello Mike, it's good to see you. We haven't met since we were at school together. Goodness me Mike! You haven't changed a bit."

Mike briefly told Paul about how he had gone to university, then trained to be an accountant, and how he had married a lovely girl called Susan. Paul related his own story and what had led him to join the Military. He was mystified by Mike's comment: "Do you ever look at other ways of making money? I'd like to run an idea past you about creating lifestyle."

That was all Paul needed. "Just now, Mike, I'm prepared to listen to anyone who has an idea that would get me out of my financial mess, legally. What is it you do?"

Mike simply replied: "I have my own business."

"Yes, Mike, but what is the business?" Mike didn't answer but asked another question: "Let me ask you something Paul, what do you think about the internet?" Paul wasn't sure but he did say that he was aware that more and more trade was being done through the internet.

"You're absolutely right, Paul. I own a profitable internet-based business. Do you see yourself retiring from the Military?"

Paul was 23. He hadn't thought about retirement. It seemed such a long way off. "All I know is that I'm not getting where I want to be in my present job."

"Then what are you looking for?" Mike enquired. "Well, I'd like to get out of debt first. Then I'd like to travel. I'd like to be able to choose a car that I like rather than one I can barely afford. I'd like to have a decent house." Paul wasn't too specific but he knew he wanted more than he had then.

"Tell me Paul, can you get out of debt and then travel, have the car of your choosing and do all these things whilst in your job on your present income?" Mike asked with a smile. Paul was quick to answer: "Well, not really. I'd need a lot more than I earn now." Mike asked another question: "Are you open to other ideas?" "Well, yes, of course I am." replied Paul emphatically.

"Paul, I can't promise you anything but in my own internet-based business we have more work than we can handle at the moment. If I could show you a way of making some serious money so that you could get out of debt, travel the world and have the car of your choosing, is that something you would want to know more about?"

Paul questioned: "Mike, do you mean I could have my own business?" "That's it." replied Mike "What's the best way to get in touch with you?" Mike handed Paul his business card and Paul wrote his phone number on it and gave the card back to Mike.

Mike continued: "Paul, I believe this is something you can do and it will give you what you're looking for. We need to get together very soon. I can give you an hour of my time to show you what the business is about. I will call you." They went their separate ways.

A couple of days later Paul was stretched out on the sofa watching TV when the phone rang. He picked it up "Hello".

"Hi Paul. This is Mike, you remember when we met you said you wanted to get out of your financial mess and travel more?"

"Hello Mike, Yes I do remember."

"Well, Susan and I could come round to your place and explain the business to you and Hannah. How about next Tuesday evening?" Paul jumped at the opportunity; "That's fine with me. Hannah and I have nothing planned then."

Chapter 1 The Initial Contact – Summary

From a nondescript background Paul dreamt of being financially free. His dream could not be fulfilled through a job. He married Hannah and they thought it could be through property ownership - until their bubble burst. School friend Mike contacted him to find that Paul was looking for something other than a job.

Points to ponder

- *Your background does not have to determine your future; your thoughts do.*

- *It's not where you come from that matters most, it's where you are heading.*

- *Will a job fulfil your dream?*

- *Friends may not be your best advisers.*

2   FINDING THE DREAM

Mike and Susan arrived precisely at 8.00 p.m. on Tuesday. "Hi Paul, it's great to see you again. This is Susan. Where's your lovely wife, Hannah?" Paul took Mike into the sitting room. "Here. Hannah, this is Mike and Susan." They greeted her enthusiastically. "Pleased to meet you Hannah." Hannah smiled shyly but with anticipation.

Mike looked around the room. "Hey Mike! What a terrific job you've done in decorating this place. Who's the artistic one?" Paul smiled and gave Hannah the credit: "Hannah did the interior design and I did the heavy work."

They all sat down and, after a short time talking about the past, Mike turned the conversation. "Now, let's get down to business; after all, that's why we're here." They all moved to the large pine table in the kitchen where they could spread out without spilling coffee over everything.

Mike started: "I can't hope to explain everything tonight. I'll cover the basics for now. Then I suggest we get together in a couple of days' time so we can do this justice." He handed Paul and Hannah a short Business Plan booklet. "We'll use this booklet to ask you a few questions and show you a business plan that could help you make some serious money. The booklet will keep me on track and you can use it to make notes as we go through."

"The first question is:"

"Who are we looking for?"

"We have found from experience that the best people to start this business, and continue building it, are *teachable*. They are willing to learn new skills in different areas. This doesn't mean that someone won't change later because this often happens."

"We are also looking for people who are *motivated* to do something; people with some 'get-up-and-go' about them."

Mike pointed to the next question in the booklet:

"Primary Motivating Factor"

"This is for both of you. Here is a list of nine reasons why you might choose to start a business. These are taken from the book: "*Questions are the Answers*" by Allan Pease. Tick the box next to your number 1 priority. You will find that just one reason stands out for you more than the others. Everyone will tick the box that is right for them."

Paul and Hannah separately ticked the same reason.

Mike pointed to the "**Why?**" Section in the booklet: "Now, can you write down why that reason is important to you?"

What is it you would both like to achieve or have?" He asked with a challenging gaze in Paul's direction.

Paul paused and thought. "I suppose, most of all, I'd like to be my own boss, without somebody else dictating my life."

"Great!" said Mike "What would you think of the idea of being a consultant, working from home, and setting your own hours? Would extra income enable you to do that?" Paul thought for a moment. Then his eyes lit up. "I have dreamed of how I could get out of the Military and make money by working for myself."

Mike could see that Paul was interested. "With this business the world's your oyster. You could travel, eat out at the best restaurants, have the cars you like. You name it, you could have what you want, or do anything you like, the choices would be yours. This business will enable you to achieve all these things. But you have to want them badly enough to put in some extra effort at the beginning. By helping other people you could build your business large enough to create sufficient cash for you to unlock your dreams."

Paul and Hannah listened as Mike explained the business further. They realized that, although they had wanted all the things he mentioned they had no plan of their own to get them. Here was his old school friend Mike, sitting with them at their kitchen table with a possible solution.

Mike continued: "This plan is about your business. The income you could earn is solely the result of your own effort. It's a two-to-five year plan as well. In two-to-five years, with consistent effort, you could achieve more than you ever would by working for someone else for 40 years."

"How?" asked Hannah.

Mike described the simplicity of building a consumer network using an internet web-site. This arrangement, as a way to access the goods and services which people already use, sounded like a good idea to Paul. He was intrigued by the concept of the efficiency and profitability that Mike had described.

At first, Hannah was not so sure about the idea. However, she did warm to it as Mike explained more: "Even though it's your own business you will not be on your own. There is a solid support system with all the help and materials that you and your organisation require."

Mike explained to them the history of the venture: "This is a global business in over seventy countries. Help is available to Business Owners from people in all of these countries. You will find you are never short of someone to turn to when you encounter difficulties, no matter where you may be promoting the business."

Mike paused to allow Paul to take in what he had just heard. "So, what do you think? You can easily register now or take time to think about it." Hannah was ready to say yes but Paul hesitated. "Let's think about it. We'll talk it over and decide in a couple of days." Hannah nodded, though she was a little disappointed. She had been won over by Mike's step-by-step approach.

Mike took a package from his briefcase. "I'll leave you this reading material and these CDs. It will help you to understand what we've been talking about; maybe it will answer some questions for you. I suggest that the most important thing for you to do now is to make three lists."

"The first one is a list of names of people you have known through your lives, right back to your school days. It can be as long as you like, the longer the better. At this stage, don't worry about where they live or whether you have their phone numbers."

"The second is a list of the things you would like to

achieve as a result of your business as you build it step-by-step."

"The third is a list of questions that you may have about the business."

Without further ado Mike departed: "See you Thursday then." He left Paul and Hannah full of questions. They discussed what they had heard that night and felt they were ready to take the first steps. They started their first list and had written 200 names in no time.

Their second list was much shorter but, for them, the most significant. They were excited at the possibilities that their own business could give them. As well as their own needs, Paul wanted to be able to provide a home for his mother. She had lived all her life in council houses and worked hard to bring up the family on her own. He felt that she deserved to live out her retirement in comfort.

Paul and Hannah also jotted down a few questions so they would remember them easily at their next meeting with Mike.

Just before 8.00 p.m. on Thursday evening Mike arrived. Very quickly they settled around the kitchen table. Mike started with a leading question: "Well, what is it that excites you most about the business?" Hannah immediately launched into her reasons. "Although I don't understand everything yet, the idea of having a new house, maybe a new car and to be able to travel really excites me."

All the time Mike was nodding and agreeing with Hannah. "Good, the most important thing for you both is to have a reason for doing this business, in other words, to fulfil a dream you've always had. Your dream needs to be bigger than all the challenges you're likely to face. In fact it certainly needs to be a lot bigger than you could possibly achieve in your present job."

After answering their questions Mike suggested that they register there and then. "Sounds like a good idea to me." said Paul. When they had completed the paperwork, registered, and placed their first product order. Mike said, "Well done! Now you've accomplished the first step I suggest you come along to your first business training meeting on Sunday afternoon. You will have an opportunity to meet other people in the business."

"What does that involve?" asked Paul.

Mike explained that the business had an excellent training and support system in which monthly training meetings were arranged at different venues. "We have people who are very experienced in this business, come along and share the lessons they've learned along the way in building their own successful businesses. We also have some great motivational speakers from outside the business. You will meet people from a variety of backgrounds and professions".

Paul and Hannah were very enthusiastic. Straight away they ordered and paid Mike for their tickets.

Chapter 2 Finding the Dream - Summary

Mike and Susan went to Paul and Hannah's house to show them the Business Plan. They spent time to let them identify and visualise their dream. Without a dream Paul and Hannah would have no motivation to start a new venture. Mike invited them to a business training meeting where they would be able to meet other people in the business.

Points to ponder

- *Establish your prospective partners' dream.*

- *Show the Business Plan.*

- *Prospective partners make big lists of names of people they know.*

- *Clarify your prospective partners' dream and get them to write it down.*

- *Follow-up within a couple of days.*

- *Register your prospective partners.*

- *Introduce the business support system.*

3 THE BUSINESS PLAN

By Sunday Paul eagerly looked forward to the business training meeting. He remembered Mike's earlier advice, "Business clothes make you look and feel like a professional." He took the advice and dressed in a suit for the occasion.

Paul and Hannah arrived at the auditorium to be greeted by several other sharp-looking, smiling people. The first couple to speak were a bank manager and his wife. He explained the business plan, outlining the principles and strategies of building a names' list, contacting people, showing them the plan and answering questions.

Three more speakers followed and gave tips about developing a successful business. For Paul, the afternoon ended all too quickly. There followed a refreshment break when Mike was able to introduce Paul and Hannah to some of his business associates.

"Phil, this is Paul and Hannah. It's their first training meeting. Perhaps you two would like to ask Phil a few questions on the business. He's building a very large business here and abroad."

Paul was keen to start the questions. "Pleased to meet you Phil. Tell me, what brought you into the business?" Phil thought for a moment before replying. "Y'know, I was doing very well financially in the city. Everything seemed to be going for me. My work days seemed to be growing longer and longer but I didn't realise what it was doing to my home life. My wife and kids had given up on me." He paused. "Then Mike introduced me to this business as a way out of the rat race. At first it seemed too good to be true. But, like you, I checked it out and found that this was

15

something that my wife, Cheryl, and I could do together. Since then we have found that our relationship has improved by leaps and bounds. Now I am able to spend more time with the kids. You see, this business isn't just about making money, although that's nice. It's about people and how we can help each other in every aspect of our lives." "Thanks a lot Phil. Good to meet you" said Paul as the call was made for everybody to return to the auditorium.

The time seemed to fly before the break was finished. There was an even greater crowd assembled. A doctor and his wife told their story of how frustrated he had been in his practice and how he found e-commerce as an alternative way of making money and creating quality time for him to spend with his family. He went on to tell their success story.

At the end of the meeting both Paul and Hannah found that the business had moved from their heads to their hearts. They knew that this business was for them and that they could make it work. The afternoon's training had opened their minds to greater things. As they walked to the car Paul had made a decision. He simply said to Hannah. "Time to get started." With a knowing smile, holding his arm: "I was hoping you'd say that." Hannah replied. He could see that she was very excited about the business.

The next step was to contact the people on their list. Deep down, though, Paul wasn't so sure; despite his excitement, he began to have second thoughts. He was hesitant and wondered if this was something he really wanted to take on: he was already involved in so many other activities. Paul played sport, coaching and playing soccer at weekends. His attitude seemed to go up and down – Paul made a note to ask Mike if this was normal. For the time being he decided to focus on the positive feelings he experienced during the business training meeting, listening to how other normal couples overcame their doubts. In the end he thought he would be positive and give the business the benefit of the doubt. Paul thought of the time in the meeting when recognition was given to all those people who had achieved a new level in their business. He thought that some of those whom he had seen being recognised for an achievement were weird. "If they can do it anyone can." Paul thought there was hope for him.

He phoned Mike and arranged a date for a meeting where they could make a few phone calls together in order to invite people to their home. Mike told him: "The great thing about this business is that, even though you are on your own you are not alone, there are other people within the business to help you."

Mike urged Paul to have a long list. "From experience, people with a long list develop a large business." Mike continued: "When you make your list be sure to include friends and family, people from your children's school, neighbours and people you have worked with in the past. Don't forget to include professionals, such as your local GP and, maybe, your accountant if you have one." Mike asked Paul not to prejudge people. "When you meet someone, you know them only by how they look and what they say. You don't know their innermost desires and dreams. You may never find out whether or not this opportunity could provide the solution they have always been looking for.

Mike continued: "When you're in conversation, just listen to what the person is saying, particularly when they talk about their job. You can always ask them if they ever look at other ways of making a living. They will soon let you know what they think. By this means you can find out their level of interest."

Paul very soon discovered that Mike was right. Being a no-nonsense chap he wanted to get to the facts straight away. This particular contacting approach, for him, was a great idea. Straight away it filtered out those who were not interested. At the beginning, Paul's style of approach was abrasive to say the least. It didn't take him long to reach this question: "Do you ever look at other ways of making money?" "Yes?" If not, "Get lost." At that time he thought it was a great way to find the people who really wanted to do more. As he practiced this approach, Paul began to learn that people reacted quite differently to this manner of questioning.

With Mike's help Paul began to develop a skill with people. His approach became more refined and less abrasive. He became a better listener. With those who said "yes" Paul confirmed appointments for them to see the business plan. He quickly realised that even those who said "no" were actually helping him reach his goal. Mike had explained that they were not rejecting Paul personally; a "yes" or a "no" was their answer just at that particular time, not forever.

As part of his continuing support for Paul and Hannah, Mike encouraged them to link into the training system. "This is the personal development training system widely used in business. As well as the training meetings we have books by well known authors and public speakers. These can help you in different areas of your life; such as managing your finances and investments, how to deal with people, how to set goals and achieve them, and how to think successfully. It's interesting that some of the authors have actually joined our business because they have seen the huge benefits that can be achieved." "These techniques are being used by many successful people in different walks of life".

Mike continued: "We have CDs from very successful people in the business. They have been through similar challenges to those which everyone faces. As they tell their stories they describe how they overcame these challenges along the way to building large, successful businesses. The benefits of this training system come from the fact that you can read the books over and over until you really know them and you can listen to the CDs time and again. The other thing, of course, is that we are all reading and hearing the same messages. Another important part of the support system we have is the mentoring from business associates and a voice messaging system to keep everyone in touch."

"How much is this education system going to cost?" asked Paul. Mike explained with a sketch showing income and costs. "You will have fixed costs that are reasonably constant each month. But you will find that your income will rise, slowly at first, until it reaches the crossover point. After that the income will rise quite steeply, provided that you structure your business in the way I suggest."

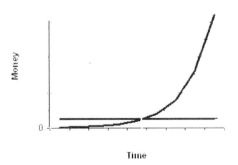

Mike suggested being with Paul and Hannah when they made the first few phone calls from their list, to help and encourage them. Although hesitant at first, Paul realised that Mike had considerable experience in handling different responses, so they agreed on the following Saturday.

That Saturday Mike arrived and they settled around the phone. Paul found himself sitting staring at it. He had a list of names and was ready to make the calls yet, somehow, he could not pick up the phone. He froze. "This is crazy." he said to Mike. "I use the phone every day at work and ask people to get together. What's the problem now?"

Finally, he managed to grip the receiver. First on the list was John from work. "Listen John, there's something important I need to ask. You remember how you wanted more time off so you and Sarah could travel before you started a family. Well, I think I've found a way we could make that happen. Are you both free on Tuesday evening to discuss this?" "Sure!" came the definite reply. "I am interested in anything that will enable us to be better off. We'll be there on the dot."

"Do you want to know the details?" Paul ventured. "No, save that for the night. You know I have absolute faith in you." "Right, see you at eight, John." As he put the receiver down Paul sighed with relief. Mike positively applauded him "Well done! That was easy enough."

Next on the list was a colleague, Jason, who played with him in the Military football team on Sundays. Jason answered straight away. "Jason, this is Paul. I wanted to see if you might be interested in an Internet-based business that offers ..." Jason wasn't so friendly. "Just a minute Paul - in the first place you know that, with my job and the football team, I just don't have time for anything else. But secondly, I can't believe you're trying to entice me into some sort of scam. Let's get it clear right now, if you want to keep my friendship then don't try and involve me in some hair-brained scheme of yours. Goodbye."

"Click" Paul was stunned. His friend had slammed the phone down on him. He felt sick in the pit of his stomach. He closed his notebook with the list and said to Mike: "This is no good. It's not going to work. I might as well give up before someone else says 'No'. Then Mike calmly asked him, "Have you got another business that will give you your dreams?" "You're right. Where do I go from here?" Paul asked.

Paul related to Mike what Jason had said. "Paul, let me ask you a couple of questions. What makes Jason such an authority on e-commerce?" Suddenly Paul brightened. "You're right. All he has done is work in a dead-end job." (Mike leaned nearer to Paul to add emphasis) "So Paul, are you going to let your future be controlled by someone else's ignorance?"

"Thanks a lot Mike, that's all I needed to hear." He picked up the phone with renewed determination to make some more phone calls. "Well done Paul! You and Hannah continue to make your calls and we should have a good meeting on Tuesday."

Tuesday evening came round very quickly. Paul had succeeded! Five couples and two singles had agreed to come to the meeting. Suddenly it didn't matter that someone had said "No".

Doctor Brown and his wife, Rosemary, arrived first, closely followed by John and Sarah. Then another couple that Paul had met only that week. A further couple had recently moved into the area and Hannah had met them in the super-market. They had agreed to come and Paul wondered why they hadn't arrived. Mike did warn him that not everyone turns up; for all sorts of reasons. Then Karen, Hannah's hairdresser arrived followed shortly by Eric, an electrician, who had been working just down the road for a few days. By 8:15 they were all seated around the kitchen table.

(The room was full but everybody enjoyed meeting one another.) Paul made the introduction just as Mike had advised him.

Mike began; "If I were to show you a business that needs no capital outlay, no red tape and no employees, would you give it careful consideration?" They all nodded in agreement. Mike then gave them all a copy of the Business Plan booklet and led them through it just as he had with Paul and Hannah. The further he went the more everyone in the room nodded in agreement. Paul and Hannah looked at each other and smiled. They felt certain their first few partners were with them on the road to freedom.

After Mike had completed the business plan they all gathered in the sitting room for questions. John and Sarah insisted on registering immediately. The other two couples wanted more information and some time to think about the idea before they committed themselves. Karen was really excited and saw how the business could help her in her salon. She was ready to register straight away. Mike went to his car and collected an information pack for each couple and one for Eric. He then arranged with them individually when, in the next 48 hours, he would return to their homes, collect the packs and answer any questions that they might have.

Paul and Hannah were elated, they felt as though they were on cloud nine. But would their bubble burst? The following morning Dr Brown phoned and asked to register. Paul was ecstatic! An hour later he received an e-mail from the other couple saying that they had decided not to proceed with the idea at that time. Paul was devastated and moaned to Hannah: "We've just begun and we've lost someone already, even before they started. What did we do wrong? They both sounded so excited last night."

Hannah consoled him the best way she could, "At least Karen will do it. Maybe it's not us but them. Why don't you call Mike and get some sound advice?"

Mike listened patiently to the tale of woe. "Where did we go wrong?" Paul asked. "You didn't." Mike replied. "People start and quit lots of things. Just think about it. How many people do you know who start diets, jobs, courses, books, even marriages and then quit when something goes wrong? Maybe their dream just isn't big enough to overcome some of their fears."

"Are you sure?" asked Paul. Mike was emphatic: "Positive! The important thing now is for you to just put this business in front of as many new people as you can. Generally you'll find that about a third of those you actually register will quit after a time; about a third will stay in for ever, use some of the products, occasionally attend meetings and, once in a while, share the plan; but about a third will be eager to build their businesses, with you or without you. You should aim to obtain 25 personal partners in your first year. After all, that's only two a month."

Paul was quite relieved; "Thanks Mike. I must learn not to let the actions and opinions of others influence my own emotions."

Mike assured Paul that his emotions would go up and down in the early days of building the business. "Remember, this business is just tough enough to separate those people who want it from those who just think they do." He continued: "When the going gets tough in any venture, whatever you do, you will find that tough times don't last, whereas tough people do. When you approach a problem or life throws a challenge at you, don't focus on the problem but keep your eyes on the solution and where you're heading.

Mike then uttered one of his many 'pearls of wisdom' "Problems always come wrapped up with solutions. You just have to find the solution."

Chapter 3   The Business Plan - Summary

At their first business training meeting Paul and Hannah learned how the business worked and how it could change people's lives. It was the event that caused Paul to make the decision to work the business. With Mike's help they made a list of people they knew and contacted some of them. Mike showed the business plan and some registered as partners with Paul and Hannah. The young couple had started building their business.

Points to ponder

- *It is your business, treat it as such: dress professionally.*

- *Learn how to meet people and make friends.*

- *Don't prejudge anyone.*

- *Move your business from your head to your heart.*

- *Make a decision to start your business.*

- *Assure yourself that you can do it.*

- *Arrange a meeting for people to hear the Business Plan.*

- *Invite everyone, even if you think they won't be interested.*

- *Use the contacting tools where appropriate.*

- *Filter out those not interested; don't waste your time and theirs.*

- *Let your emotions be driven by your own dreams, not by external influences.*

- *Keep close contact with your mentor or coach.*

- *Put your business in front of as many people as you can.*

4   BUILDING THE BUSINESS

The following Monday Mike met Paul and Hannah in town for coffee. Mike gave them some advice on how to run and structure their business for profit. After coffee was served he wasted no time: "The business is based on a sliding scale." He said. "It's reasonable to aim for the first business level in your first month. One simple plan I recommend to new people is to use some, and share some."

"First, we use products from our own business. You have a whole range of items to meet your family needs. You will find that, if you are loyal to your business, your business will be loyal to you. Treat your business like your own on-line supplier and tell your friends and acquaintances at the same time."

"The second method is; we share. We do this by registering people as associates. These people are not interested in building a business, as such, but do like to use the products. They can purchase their own goods and services directly from the supplier at wholesale prices."

"If you follow this pattern right from the start and teach your business partners to do the same, you will build a sound business. The size of the income streams that you develop will depend on how good you become at helping your new business partners to redirect their shopping."

"As you start each new business partner, either you or Hannah should lead them through their 'new store'. Show them how to go on-line, use the phone, study the literature and teach them how to place the orders themselves. Then show them how to use the products. It's important for Hannah to teach the ladies."

After their meeting with Mike, the couple could not wait to place their first order through the web-site. Paul realised how fortunate he was to have Mike as his mentor.

Their business began to grow. Then one day Hannah told Paul that she was expecting. They were thrilled at the news. It meant that Paul had another very good reason to work harder at building the business. Nine months later, when Timothy was born, their first dream, or goal, was realised. Earlier, they had agreed that Hannah would give up work and look after Timothy full time. Not long after Hannah had adjusted to her new role in motherhood she found she was expecting again, this time with Matthew. They were growing both their business and their family!

Paul and Hannah's business had started very slowly at first. They kept going and introduced some of their friends and people they met as new business partners. After eleven months of consistent effort they found they were making steady progress.

Their income from the business had risen to almost £3,000 a month.

Paul was beginning to identify key leaders within his group. They all benefited from the monthly goal-setting sessions that they had together. This 'goal setting' gave them all a sense of direction and purpose. They were working together as a team. To be effective as a leader Paul was very keen to work closely with other more successful people in the business. In this way he was able to pass down to the leaders in his group the valuable experience and knowledge that he gained.

Mike had also taught Paul that, with the help of others in this business around the world, he could develop his business in other countries - more income streams! Mike had explained that the only limitation to the size of their business would be how far they could stretch their minds. The more he saw and understood about the business the more Paul realised how big it could become.

On one occasion, a client remarked to Paul in conversation. "You certainly seem to be doing well with your business, Paul. Mike says you make a very good student." Paul remembered something Mike had said. "When the student is ready a teacher will appear."

"Yes, I'm really grateful to have Mike as my coach in this business. With his experience he seems to be able to lead me through the pitfalls and keep me on track."

Paul arrived home one evening to find Timothy asleep and Hannah with her feet up. They were talking about how quickly the business had allowed Hannah to "retire". Then Paul gasped: "Do you realise that, only a couple of months ago, I was tempted not to continue with the business. It makes me shudder now to think about it. Mike did warn me that this could happen to anyone at any stage. Do you remember that Friday evening when Joe phoned and asked me to go 'down south' for a soccer weekend. I desperately wanted to go but we had a business meeting coming up and I needed to prepare for it. I was very tempted to go with Joe and forget the whole business. Then I thought of all our dreams, phew! That was a close shave." They hugged each other.

Paul thought about what Mike had said to him. "When you are in real doubt, at a crossroad, and don't know which way to turn read this little book. It's about building pipelines." Paul had stuffed it in a drawer in their bedroom. That night he found it. Burke Hedges' book *"The Parable of the Pipeline"*. He read the whole book in one sitting. He thought it was a gem and it really helped him to focus on what he was doing.

Paul began to understand how his business was comparable to the different pipelines in the book. Each new business partner he registered was effectively a new pipeline, a separate source of income for Paul and the partner. That's why Mike had advised him to start as many as 25 partners or more in the first year. With Paul's help – and Mike's - each partner would build their own business for their own reasons and dreams, and achieve their own success.

Needless to say, Paul had decided not to go to the soccer weekend and planned his next meeting instead. Had he not done so who knows? Hannah might have been going back to work leaving Timothy with a childminder.

Paul realised that *"The Parable of the Pipeline"* had a real parallel in his own town. A man named George was asked by a neighbour if he would lend him his car for a journey that he thought his own car wouldn't manage.

George was happy to help out. While his neighbour was away George decided to buy another car just for hiring out. This succeeded to the point where he bought another, and another. Each car became a new income stream. Then he decided to repeat his business in another town, and another.

Paul realised that his own business was not in vehicles and depots, nor in water transport and construction, it was in developing relationships through business partners and helping them to build their own businesses. His time, effort and all the travelling were investments in his future, to make sure that each new business partnership he set up developed a new income stream.

Chapter 4   Building the Business - Summary

Paul and Hannah started to use products from their business. They encouraged their business partners to do the same. As their business grew Paul and some of the partners worked closely as a team to the benefit of all in the group. Paul's business grew steadily as he added each new partner.

Points to ponder

- *Use the products and services from your own business.*
- *Teach your business partners how to order and use the products to duplicate your pattern.*
- *Be a good student and teacher.*
- *Identify key leaders in your business.*
- *Work closely with successful people.*
- *Think BIG!*
- *Don't be distracted from your goals.*
- *Your business is building pipelines or income streams.*
- *Remember that short-term pain equals long-term gain.*

5   DUPLICATION

At their next meeting Paul enthusiastically told Mike how he had read *"The Parable of the Pipeline"* and could see the relevance to his business.

"Yes," Mike replied. "Most people are 'bucket carriers', in what is otherwise known as the 'Time-for-Money Trap'." He explained that the problem with being paid for time is that, when you stop putting in the time, the money stops coming in."

"You see, Paul, it is important to consider what would happen if you couldn't work in your job for any reason. The bills would continue. What if you did not have an alternative lifeline to protect you and your family? So what's the answer? A pipeline of course!" Mike continued, "Additional income streams enable you to escape the 'Time-for-Money Trap.' If you work for other people, when the work dries up, so does the lifestyle. It seems to me crystal clear that building other income streams is the only way to create true financial freedom for yourself and your family."

Paul was beginning to see clearly the connection between building his business and building pipelines.

Mike asked a question: "Now, Paul, the question for you to think about is; how do you put your new business plan into action?" To answer his own question Mike explained the principle of leverage. "Think about it. You could type an invitation to an event and type it again for every person you invited. Alternatively, you could type the invitation once, without names, and then photocopy it or print it as many times as you like. This is leverage, just as in printing books. Best selling authors write the book just once and it can be printed millions of times to satisfy the demand. Through royalties each copy of the book gives an income to the author. A new book becomes a new income stream."

"That, Paul, is the power of leverage. Leverage multiplies the effort we make, hundreds or even thousands of times. That is what makes it such a powerful business tool."

Mike expanded on this theme: "Another idea which you will have come across in school is also linked to leverage. It's called the doubling concept, or 'geometric progression', which is the technical term for it, and it embodies the notion of leverage. Here's a good example. Supposing you registered just one person into your business each month and you taught each of your business partners to do the same."

Paul considered the concept thoughtfully. On the face of it the idea didn't seem too bad. Mike could see Paul weighing up the situation. "Let's draw it out on a chess board and you will see it's just phenomenal. Each square is a month. "Just the first two rows alone would go like this:"

1	2	4	8	16	32	64	128
256	512	1024	2048	4096	8192	16384	32768

Mike continued: "In the first month there is just you. In the second month you register one partner, that makes two of you in your business. The third month you register another and the first partner also registers one. Your business now has four partnerships."

"To leverage your money by employing the doubling concept is simple. Instead of just saving in an ordinary current account in the bank, what do we do?" Without waiting for Paul he answered his question; "You invest it and leave the money to double or, to put it another way, to earn compound income. For example: Let's say you put £100 on deposit and during the first year it grows by an amount, say 10%. The second year it will start off at £110 because the income has been added to your investment. At the end of the second year it will be £121. Growing at this rate it would have doubled in seven years. This is how self-made millionaires become wealthy. They build their own pipelines by investing some of their income and letting it compound year after year."

Paul chipped in: "What if I haven't got the money to invest?" Anticipating the question, Mike replied with a smile: "Then just do what you have a lot of: leverage your time."

Mike explained: "During the early days of building your business you are investing your time to achieve both time savings and additional income. If you are consistent you will reach the point where you are no longer dependent on a job with a boss and all that goes with it. You will be your own independent business owner.

Chapter 5   Duplication - Summary

Paul learned the benefit of building his own business for himself and his family. Mike taught him the principles of time leverage and the doubling concept. He found that, as he invested time into his business, so it grew.

Points to ponder

- *The principle of leverage.*

- *The doubling concept.*

- *In your business you invest time in the early years.*

- *Your time is repaid handsomely in later years.*

6   E-COMMERCE

Paul was steadily building the business with new partners being added regularly. He showed the business plan to Nick and Helen. They were very enthusiastic. Nick was a decorator and Helen a secretary. They knew that Nick's income was totally dependent on his being at work each day.

Paul was putting into practice what he had learnt from Mike. He was giving Nick and Helen a training session on the business and the internet.

"You see, Nick," Paul continued; "the beauty of time leverage is that we have all been given the same amount of time. Just think for a moment what we could accomplish in our lives if we used a couple of hours each evening and at the weekends to build income streams. We now have available a fantastic time leveraging tool, probably the best that's ever been. E-commerce is an amazing tool and it is the ultimate tool for time leverage."

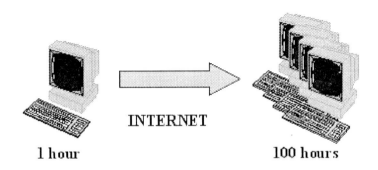

INTERNET

1 hour   100 hours

"So, there we have it, e-compounding, the ultimate income stream. Yes, the internet is a system where millions of people all over the globe, each connected via a computer, are able to communicate or buy and sell to each other. All this is for the price of a local telephone call. Nick, it's mind boggling!"

Mike went on another step: "At last, through the internet we can realise our dreams. But even the internet has drawbacks. It's too big, too crowded, too confusing."

"According to experts, e-commerce sites face three major challenges:

1. They need more traffic.
2. They need more sales.
3. They need more repeat business.

"To succeed on the internet an e-commerce site needs loyal customers. By loyal customers I mean people who have a reason to buy regularly from that same site week after week and month after month, instead of once in a blue moon." Helen was puzzled; "But Paul, how do we get people to do this regular buying, week after week on the net? How is it done?"

"That's a good question Helen" Paul was ready for this.

"The answer is to establish solid relationships with normal families and that's where you and Nick can build your income streams. In your normal dealings you recommend products and services all day, every day, for free. People shop and buy based on your recommendations. A conventional shop doesn't pay you for promoting its products even if you do recommend it to your friends. Word of mouth advertising has been used for years, but doesn't usually pay you anything. However, you can now advertise just as easily and be paid for it! You just recommend to your friends the goods and services that you can provide through your business. They may want to join as business partners. If they do then you, your business partners and your clients all benefit. It's a win-win situation for everybody."

"This is how it is done. The e-commerce company's role is to provide the website, take the on-line orders, ship the products direct to the consumers and process the credit or debit cards. The company handles all the accounting. The company gets loyal customers who return to the site again and again and, in return, they pay us what you could call referral fees. So, to sum up, you get paid to compound your time and relationships via the internet and you build yourself the ULTIMATE PIPELINE!"

Nick was doubtful. "I understand that, Paul, but how can I use this to make money?" "Well Nick, your goal is to find just one person each month who is interested in their own financial future and security and you become his mentor or coach."

"You just keep repeating the process. By the end of the first year, your business would have personally partnered with 12 different people, one new person each month. Let's assume that each one of them partnered with one new person each month, as well. This is where the power of duplication and compounding kicks in. By the end of 12 months, your network could compound to 4,096 affiliated, independent partnerships!"

"You will be paid by the internet company an amount proportional to the total value of goods purchased by you and your affiliated partners."

Paul was excited. The December Business Training Meeting was approaching and they had almost reached the business level they had set themselves as their first goal. They arrived at the Convention Centre early in the afternoon. At one o'clock sharp the speakers were introduced and the crowd came alive. The discussions centred round the concept of working with people, managing their finances and other tips and techniques for building the business. Paul, however, was looking forward to the evening session as he and Hannah would be going on stage for the first time as new business level achievers. Their business had reached the point where they were able to tell their story. The evening session came and, all too quickly, they found themselves on stage relating the way their business had grown, including some of the challenges they faced.

"We're Paul and Hannah Evans. I am a Military sports coach and Hannah has given up her job to look after our sons, Timothy and Matthew ..." Paul only half heard the applause of 2,000 people as they walked off the stage. But it did feel so good. Mike was waiting at the foot of the stage and gave them both hugs and congratulations.

In the next few months after their first opportunity to speak Paul and Hannah were very busy. John and his wife were doing almost as well. They were both aiming for the same level. Paul decided to step up the pace so they could achieve it together.

They were earning about £4,000 a month and Paul decided to give up work. He wanted to be in control of what he was doing. There is a rank system in the Military. He remembered a particular officer who was always very grumpy. Paul nervously approached the officer's building and knocked at his office door. He thought to himself: "Well, I don't have to be intimidated by this guy, after all I'm leaving."

He knocked on the door. The officer didn't even look at Paul. He had his head down. "What do you want? I hear you want to leave, Evans. Let me give you a piece of advice." Paul interrupted: "Excuse me, Sir, before you start I don't need your advice. I will take advice from someone who earns more money than I do. I now earn twice as much money in my spare time as you do, working full time." Paul walked out of the door and has never looked back.

The following day Paul went in to collect his belongings from the office. As he walked out of the building for the last time he saw Mike and John, with their wives, standing by a limousine with Hannah and the boys seated inside. They had a bottle of champagne and six glasses. After the toasts were over Paul and his family climbed into the chauffeur-driven limo. "Where to?" the driver asked. Paul stuck his head out of the window and announced to the world: "To the best restaurant in town. We're celebrating."

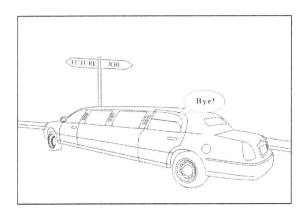

During the meal, Paul remembered some advice he and Hannah had been given when they first started their business. Advice from well-meaning friends, "You could lose all your money." Paul had thought; "I have no money. Nothing equals nothing so I'll give it a go." They said he would lose his car. He lost his rusty Ford Capri for a 500 Mercedes soft top, a Jaguar and a 4-Wheel Drive for Hannah.

Paul was even told he would lose his house. He didn't have a house. They lived in married quarters which Paul and Hannah were quite happy to give up for a seven-bedroom house with an indoor swimming pool. He liked having an indoor swimming pool. He could go for a swim at any time and wear anything. Fantastic!

Other statements from their friends had included: "They wouldn't be able to have any holidays." Since Paul and Hannah started their business they have enjoyed over forty holidays, many being the result of the free travel incentives through their business. They now have a lot of genuine friends around the world who are helping them to achieve their goals and dreams.

Knowing what they have achieved Paul is amused to think that even some of their closest friends and family told them that they would not make it. They had heard them all but hadn't felt the need to listen.

Chapter 6   E-commerce - Summary

Paul taught his business partners the lessons he had learned from Mike, particularly the vital role the internet plays in time leverage. His business was "high tech" through the internet and "high touch" through building relationships. Paul and Hannah experienced recognition through their business and the joy of Paul's last day at work.

Points to ponder

- *Successful E-commerce sites have:*

    A user-friendly content.

    People making regular visits to the site – community.

    Regular orders from the community - commerce.

- *Build solid relationships.*

- *Recommend products and services.*

- *You earn by referring customers to the site.*

- *Find people who are genuinely interested in their financial future.*

- *Become a mentor or coach.*

- *Think and plan when the income from your business will allow you to give up your job with a boss.*

- *Watch how you respond to negative people.*

7   YOUR LAST DAY AT WORK

The big event arrived. This was the day that Paul and Hannah would be guest speakers at a large business conference. This would be the day they could announce that they had achieved their big goal.

The couple boarded a helicopter. As they landed in London a limousine arrived to take them to the arena. As they arrived the doors were opened for them and they were escorted to the VIP courtesy lounge behind the stage. They were provided with refreshments and were able to watch the programme in progress on closed-circuit TV.

As they stood at the entrance to the stage behind a pulled-back curtain, Paul peered out into the audience. He saw the faces of strangers who, over the years of building his business, had become close friends. He saw members of his family who had supported them in their quest. Timothy and Matthew were in the audience. Hannah's sister was taking care of them. Timothy, the older one was very aware of what the business meant. He was aware of the money it brought in but, most of all, the freedom it gave the family. He knew his mum and dad had lots of friends phoning, coming to the house and going on trips with them.

Soon it was their turn to go on stage. As if in a dream, they walked on. Mike introduced them: "Ladies and Gentlemen, please help me give a tremendous welcome to successful business owners: Paul and Hannah Evans."

As they took the stage amidst the roar of the crowd, they looked up and saw their names in lights, they were overjoyed at the truly celebratory event that seemed to be just for them.

Paul opened his speech:

"This is our story. All I can say is that I truly believe that becoming wealthy through this business is an option available to everyone, it is just a matter of personal choice. Are you up for it? I acknowledge that the growth of our business is the result of several factors that we had in our favour; a good relationship with our mentors and the groups we were helping and a clear purpose, which I will refer to as a dream. We had a dream worth fighting for, as well as the guidance and continuous support from Mike, our friend and mentor."

"Everyone building this business will experience different rates of growth in their businesses due to all sorts of reasons: personal issues such as poor self-image, fear, marriage challenges, or lack of a really significant dream. Any of these, and other obstacles, can be overcome through reading the right books, listening to inspirational CDs, attending training meetings, mixing with like-minded people and, I must say, having an experienced and knowledgeable mentor. They say that when the student is ready the teacher will appear. This has been so true in our case. Not just Mike alone but the training organisation has provided counsel and support throughout the growth of our business."

"I checked with Mike before we came on stage and he was happy for me to say that, as we have grown our business, we have reached a level where we make more money than he does at present. He is very pleased for us that we have reached this far in the business. He is also pleased that the income stream he has, as a result of helping us to develop our business, is large and secure. This is one of the great things about this business, everybody can grow at their own pace. When you are your own boss you can decide how much time and effort you are prepared and able to put into your own business."

"I realise that my business is like a plant, it can either grow or die. It is very difficult to keep it in exactly the same healthy state. You could say it is also like a garden, even though it grows beautiful flowers, it does need constant attention. That's why I have always encouraged people in my group to keep their minds healthy for growth, a bit like the soil in the garden. Rich soil produces rich results. In the early days I found that the easiest way for me to do this was to rely on the training system of books, CDs and the monthly training meetings that were essential to my personal growth and that of the business. It was at the training meetings where I met a lot of people in my group for the first time. The business expanded quickly because some of our business partners understood duplication. They developed their own businesses, introducing new business partners and bringing them to the training meetings."

"The results from your business system are very predictable and relate directly to the amount of effort you and your mentor put into building the business. You just have to make the decision, be willing to become a student of the system and put in the effort. In time you will find the results will come. It is there for every one of you. When you have minor setbacks always remind yourself that it is only temporary. You can put up with anything for a couple of years. I'll tell you what, it beats the forty-year system of working for a boss only to find you have little or no reward at the end. For all of you who are under 40, just think for a moment what your pension will be like after you've finished forty years in a job with a boss."

"This business system is very simple. We just learned from our mentor. With his guidance we duplicated what he showed us. Finally we taught our business partners what we had learned."

"One major thing we have learned through building this business is that our thinking and our habits have changed significantly. An old Portuguese proverb says; "Change yourself,

43

change your fortunes." Certainly, this has happened to us. There is an analogy with an elastic band; when it is expanded and released it doesn't go back to its original shape. I feel we would find it difficult to think as small as we previously did as our minds, like the elastic band, have been stretched."

"We have been aware of changes in the way the business works now, compared to when we started. It is now easier to build this business using current technology such as e-mail, mobile phones and on-line shopping. I am convinced that there has never been a better time to build this business than right now."

"Even though we have developed a successful business, we still value our family time as being essential. I now have the time to keep fit and pursue my hobby - playing golf with my two boys on some of the most exclusive courses around the world."

"Our lifestyle has completely changed; in only two-and-a-half years from starting to build our business. We will never have to work for anyone else again. It's great! You can get up in the morning just when you want and not be governed by alarm clocks. We are now full-time parents. This is the best thing that has happened to us; now we are always there for our children."

"When you are earning a few thousand a month out of this business, wouldn't it be nice if you could go into work one day and say to your boss that you were planning to go on an extended holiday and it might be better if he found someone else to do your work, just in case you decided not to come back."

Paul took a piece of paper from his pocket.

"Your resignation letter could read something like this:"

"Dear Boss,

I really have enjoyed working for you and your company over the last few years (you can put in your own number) but I have now arrived at the point where I feel I must release you as my boss.

Please don't take it personally but I have reached the time in my life, even though I'm only 28, where, for several reasons (a few are listed below), it would be better for both of us if you were to appoint somebody more deserving of my job.

- The working hours with your company start a little too early in the morning and finish a little too late in the afternoon.

- I would prefer to spend more time with my family than with you. No offence intended.

- For some time now I have felt that the holiday arrangements with your company are a little restrictive, whereby I only have six weeks annual leave, and you say when I can take it.

- Your company pension plan will leave me quite broke when I retire after forty years of loyal and faithful service.

- The salary you pay me is insufficient for me to live in the house or take the holidays of my choosing.

- Your company health-care plan does not include my parents and my wife's parents. (I feel that I should look after them a bit better in their twilight years.)

- The company car you provide doesn't have the luxury I deserve.

If you are happy for me to leave this afternoon it would be most convenient for me. You see, a limousine has been arranged to collect me at lunchtime.

Yours sincerely,

"I'm not suggesting that you should be rude in your letter. After all, you never know when you might be asked if you will let him/her join your business in the future!"

"To sum up, all I can say is don't give up and, if you are finding that you are moving on, don't be afraid to retire from your normal job, whatever that is. I did and I've never looked back."

"I will pass you over to Hannah to give her an opportunity to tell you what building the business has meant to her."

Hannah nervously took the microphone from Paul.

"For me, the best thing has just been to see our children become more confident and more sociable. They know what they want out of life. When I was their age I had no idea what I wanted to do or be."

"One day we took Timothy to a car showroom so he could see his dream car. He was talking to the sales representative there, discussing the different makes of cars. Timothy turned to me and said; "Mum have you ever been close to a Ferrari?" "No." I replied. He opened the door and I peered inside. It was the first time I had seen inside a Ferrari. Then Timothy said: "Mum, can you just visualise it. Can you picture yourself in one of these cars?"

"I said, "Yes, wow! Goodness, I'm going to get envious looks from everyone."

"Mum, all you have to do is build the business." That shut me up. He went on to say, "That's all you have to do. When I grow up I'm going to build the business and buy a Ferrari. If you do the same, you can have one too." I said, "Fine. OK" Already Timothy and Matt know exactly the sort of house they want to live in, the nice cars they want. Timothy said to me, "Just imagine, mum, all those women chasing after me!"

"Our children are focused. So build it for your children." Hannah handed the microphone back to Paul.

Paul concluded their speech:

"I remember when we told our story for the first time at one of the business training meetings. Hannah, you tell them how we met."

Hannah took the microphone again: "When I first met Paul I saw him as a challenge. He was very good looking and very popular with the ladies. My friends said I'd never manage to date him. At the time I thought there's no harm in trying! Now, here I am, blessed with this fantastic husband." Everyone applauded.

Paul took back the microphone. "I must tell you about an

incident with our bank. I remember a conversation with the manager before we started our business. I asked him for an overdraft. He was very off-hand with his reply "I'll let you know next week."

"Later, when our business was thriving, the manager phoned me: "Congratulations, your account looks very healthy. I'd like to take you out to dinner and a show. I know you like soccer, maybe you'd like to see an international game or Cup match?" I replied, "Thanks, I'll let you know next week." From then on, we focussed our efforts on building our very own business." Paul and Hannah left the stage to a standing ovation.

Chapter 7   *Your Last day at work - Summary*

Paul and Hannah's big day arrived when they could speak at a large business training meeting and tell their story. They related how the training system had helped them and their children in their personal development and business. Light-heartedly Paul suggested a resignation letter. They were able to look back on some of their experiences as they built their business.

Points to ponder

- *"Change yourself, change your fortunes."*

- *This is a learn, do, teach business.*

- *One of your goals could be to speak at a major function.*

- *Another could be to get out of your job with a boss.*

- *Plan the date for your last day of work.*

- *Have clearly in mind what you will do on that day.*

- *Write your "retirement" letter in a pleasant way.*

- *Build your business for your children.*

8 PROFESSIONALS BUILD THE BUSINESS

Paul and Hannah had their first opportunity to host a major training function. He took the microphone:

"Now, ladies and gentlemen, please give a rousing welcome to our next speakers, a couple with professional backgrounds who have built a large, profitable business. Let me introduce you to Dr Peter Brown and his wife Dr Rosemary Brown."

A couple in their early forties came on stage. The husband took the microphone and began to speak.

"When we saw this business we could see the potential of developing extra security for us and our family. Medicine does provide us with a good lifestyle and a reasonable income. However, we realised that it was dependent on both of us having to put in the effort and work for it. If anything happened to either of us we could never maintain our lifestyle without working one way or another. Our major purpose to develop our own business was to provide that extra security for our family."

"We felt that this business offered us a much better quality of life. We knew it would give us the extra time to spend together with our family. Being in the medical profession does place extra demands on our time. We have a family and a reasonable income but we did not have the time to spend with them."

"Don't misunderstand me, we had all the benefits of a good life, such as good schools and fantastic holidays, but we found it difficult to spend the time together - quality time - so the children did actually lose out until we developed this business. Now we are able to include an important dimension in their development, which is learning life skills from us, their parents."

"Another benefit we saw in this business was for us to maintain a standard of life style through into retirement. Incidentally, we are able to retire at a much younger age than we would have been able to do in our careers. We know many doctors who have retired and have had to limit their lifestyles, some have had to sell their lovely homes and move into smaller ones, euphemistically called 'downsizing' Those that wanted to travel could not do so in the present climate of the health profession. Many doctors will be in a position when they retire that they must continue working. To be quite frank, when you have worked hard all your life you would normally expect a reasonably comfortable retirement. We do not feel that medicine would give us that these days."

"Lastly, we saw it as a new way to help others. We both went into medicine because we enjoy helping people. But, when you've been in a job for a long time, you reach a stage when many of the things you do become repetitive. To some extent healthcare professionals are victims of their own success. There are more and more people being treated medically and there is an ever increasing older population. Then we find that there is more work to do with insufficient people to do it. We are endeavouring all the time to catch up with what is expected of us. So the fresh challenge of this business was very welcome to us. When we saw the business plan we jumped at it and have been very pleased with the way it's worked out."

The doctor handed the microphone back to Paul.

"Peter, I'd like to make an observation," Paul said to the doctor. "You mentioned that you could not maintain a good lifestyle unless you and your wife continued working." I mention that in the literature I give to people when I show the business plan. It's about building pipelines. You have all read Burke Hedges' book *"The Parable of the Pipeline"* and the story of the

50

two friends who built a pipeline instead of carrying buckets. Once the pipeline was complete the brothers did not have to carry buckets anymore The water flowed whether they worked or not. It flowed while they ate. It flowed while they slept. The more the water flowed into the village, the more the money flowed into the boys' pockets."

Paul paused. There were loud cheers and applause.

"This business is very similar because it is based on e-compounding. When you have built the business you make money, whether you actually work or not. You can be on a beach in the Bahamas and the money will still be flowing into your bank account. That's the beauty and the power of this business."

The doctor replied; "It's funny you should say that. It was *"The Parable of the Pipeline"*, the book you lent us when we started our business, and about the story of the pipeline that prompted me to investigate the business more closely. After reading these words of wisdom I found them such a source of inspiration that I decided to give it a chance. As it says in the book, "If you don't try something, you will never know whether you will succeed in it or not."

Paul asked again; "Peter, another question is this: Do you think a business like this would appeal to other doctors and professionals or is it how you personally feel about it?

The doctor was quite emphatic: "I certainly feel that other doctors and people in many other jobs, as well as professions, are looking for other ways to make a living. One of the major issues for many people is time. As professionals we have to be very committed. We have a twenty-four hour responsibility. In the same way lawyers, accountants and teachers all have huge responsibilities in their different fields. Therefore, I think this is an ideal business to develop within that sort of framework. It is essential for people to develop the business alongside whatever work they do. This is a real business which gives a real return on the time invested."

Paul moved towards the microphone. "One concern I have, Peter, and perhaps you might put my mind at rest about it, is that, with the responsibility of being a doctor in the community and having that sort of prestige, you obviously need to be alert in your work. Do you feel that building this business has affected your performance in any way at all as a doctor?"

Dr Brown gazed at Paul, moved closer to the microphone and replied. "Oh absolutely, in a very positive way it has affected us. With any business you go through a learning process and the good thing about this one is that the skills that we have learned; particularly with respect to people skills and communication skills, has certainly helped us in what we do. Also we have developed an empathy towards people and understand more where they are coming from. That certainly helps us in dealing with people in a holistic sort of way, rather than just looking at the disease."

"Thank you Doctor Brown."

Chapter 8   Professionals Build the Business - Summary

A doctor and his wife related their story on how they had built their business and how it had changed their lives. In questioning the doctor it was clear to Paul that people from all walks of life were keen to build the business. He had found people from all trades and professions in his own business who were enthusiastically building their businesses.

Points to ponder

- *Even professional people can be looking for more.*

- *People from all backgrounds build this business.*

- *Everyone has their own reason to build this business.*

- *Busy people build this business to gain time.*

9   A DREAM FULFILLED

The telephone rang. Paul picked up the receiver. "Hello."

"Hi Paul, it's Ron here, you remember, we met at the weekend conference in Memphis, Tennessee?"

"Hello Ron. Yes I do remember, that was a terrific event. The people and the sessions really helped us move our business on by leaps and bounds. How can I help?"

"Well, Paul, it has been suggested that you and Hannah might be willing to come over here and speak at our weekend training meeting in October. What do you think?"

Paul was nervous at the thought of speaking at such a huge gathering. But, at the same time, he felt honoured that they should be asked.

"Thanks Ron, I'm really honoured to think that we should be invited to speak at your major event. What subject would you like us to speak on?"

"Paul, you know that the driving force for anybody to succeed in this business is that inner motivation, the dream. I guess that you've had quite a few of your dreams fulfilled since you started. How about 'Your Dreams Can Come True'?"

"Sounds good. OK, Ron, I'll tell Hannah. She will be pleased. She always likes a good reason to buy new outfits. Thanks very much for asking."

"Bye then, Paul, talk to you later."

"Bye Ron." Paul put the phone down and smiled. Another dream is about to be unlocked. Paul and Hannah speaking at an international meeting! "Wait 'till I tell Hannah." He mused to himself.

The event drew near. The young couple had received their first-class air tickets, they had been booked into a five star hotel, chauffeur driven limousines to and from the airports, all expenses paid. Wow!

"Please help me to give a rip-roaring welcome to the stage, my UK friends and yours, true leaders in this business and great motivational speakers: Paul and Hannah!"

Paul just could not have expected such an enthusiastic ovation.

"Thanks for that warm welcome and introduction"

"It really has been a great privilege for us to build this business and do the things that we had only dreamed about. We'll tell you about some of the 'champagne moments' that have served as beautiful memories. We remember a ski trip near Lake Tahoe, nestling high in the mountains, on the border between California and Nevada. At that time the boys were six and four. We went to a place called Heavenly. We can understand why it's called that. We travelled up to about 10,000 feet above sea level in a cable car. We could see the whole panoramic view. It was so magnificent. The brilliant blue lake, with iridescent colours on its surface was laid out before us. We could see the blazing sun, and the mountain caps covered with virgin-white snow. It was just breathtaking and so clear we could see for miles. I looked over at Matthew and Timothy. Timothy turned to me and said: "Hey Dad, this is the life." No one forgets moments like that. It would have been impossible for me to achieve this much as a military Physical Training Instructor."

"We remember going to places like Bermuda and the Bahamas, completely free of charge, to help us develop our business. We enjoyed the trip so much that we went again with the children at our own expense."

"We have discovered that there are so many choices we can make as a result of developing this business. We went on a yacht which normally costs 10,000 dollars a day. With this business we were able to go free. Once we stopped at a port in the Caribbean and strangers were photographing the yacht before we sailed. On the deck I couldn't help thinking: "It's ours for a little while." Only four couples who developed large businesses were able to sail on it for that week. It's great to be in the position to have these trips."

"We could talk about the different cars, the houses or the things that we have been able to achieve through this business, but that wouldn't really help you. The bottom line is, what are your dreams? What are you going to do with this business? You see, you have to ask yourself, if you don't do it, who loses out? What if it did work and you didn't do it? Surely, if you don't check it out, you would always wonder if it was worth checking out. By attending the training meetings and listening to people with genuine experience of building this business, you can make the right choice."

"Whether you decide to do the business or not, you owe it to yourself to check it out thoroughly. By spending one Sunday afternoon you could find out for yourself. You must realise that, if two people like us in our early twenties, lacking confidence, no qualifications, no business experience or skills in dealing with people and no credibility, can become financially free in a few years then you can do it too. The vehicle is far more developed today with the internet."

"Just imagine and dream what you can do with this business."

Chapter 9   A Dream Fulfilled - Summary

One of Paul's dreams was to speak at an international gathering of business owners. This came into being "out of the blue" from a telephone call. Paul and Hannah could not contain their excitement. A new outfit for Hannah, a great story for Paul to tell, and first class travel, all expenses paid. They were able to relate some of the many travel experiences that they had enjoyed with their two sons. Then Paul turned the attention from his story and challenged the audience: What would they be able to do if they decided to work the business?

Points to ponder

- What are your dreams?

- Would you change anything if you knew you couldn't fail?

- Do you have a plan to reach your dreams?

- What sort of people would you like to travel with?

- This business is simple and relatively easy.

- It worked for Paul and Hannah. Would it work for you?

- It will work when you change your thinking and behaviour.

- Do you want the results enough to make the change?

10 CONCLUSION – UNLOCK YOUR DREAMS

Paul and Hannah succeeded in their business because they wanted to.

Their aspirations and dreams were so big that they made the business their priority over other leisure pursuits.

They knew nothing about the business when they started but they were good students.

The training and counselling received through the support system was enough to stretch them without overwhelming them.

They learned how to get on with people and develop real, lasting, friendships.

They followed a proven and tested pattern that had been used by many successful people before them.

They had clear short-term, medium-term and long-term goals along the way and they focused on them as they progressed.

They didn't let challenges and disappointments hold them back.

They learned how to overcome objections.

The business is simple but not one which everyone will dare to do.

Paul and Hannah are still unlocking their dreams.